The shopping

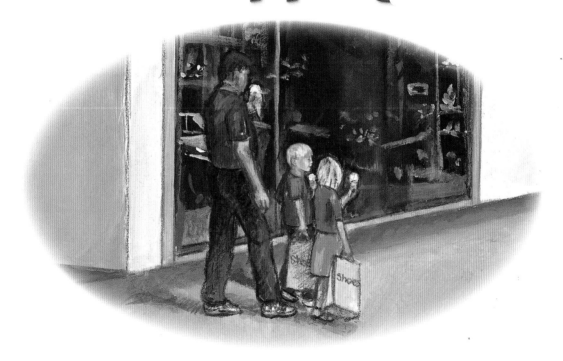

We went

to the shopping mall.

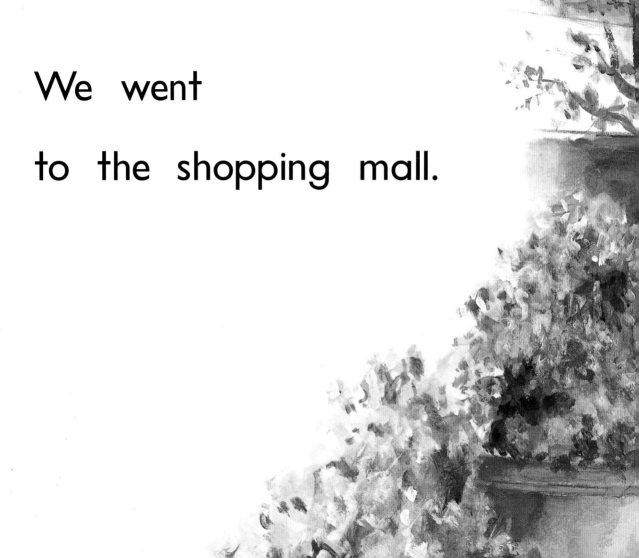

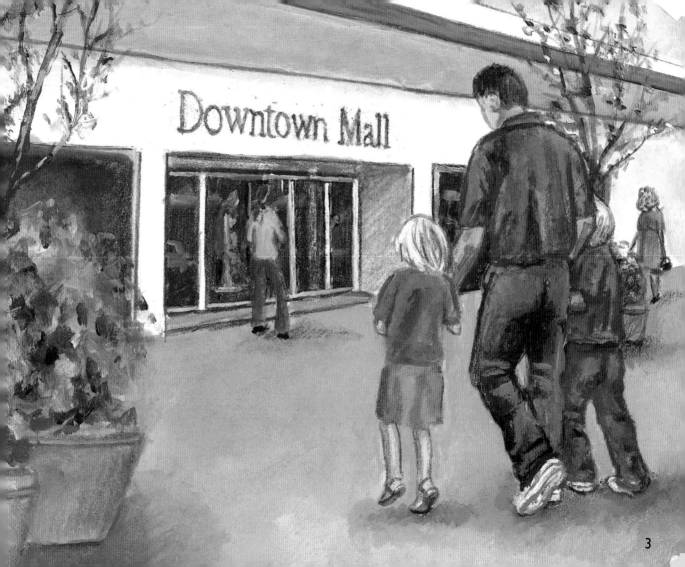

We went

in the doors.

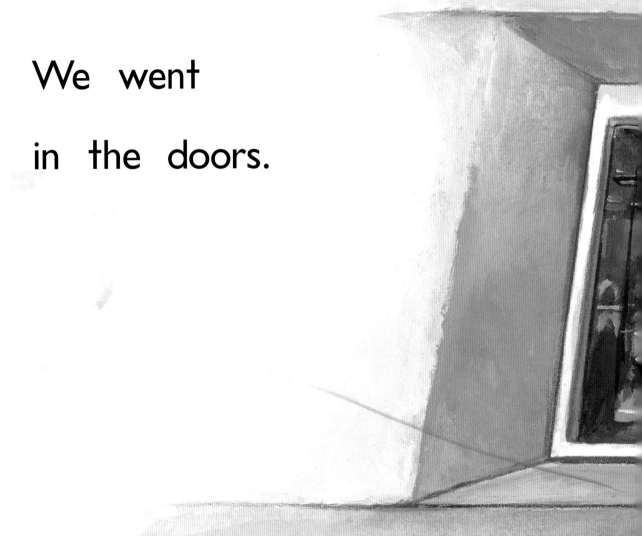

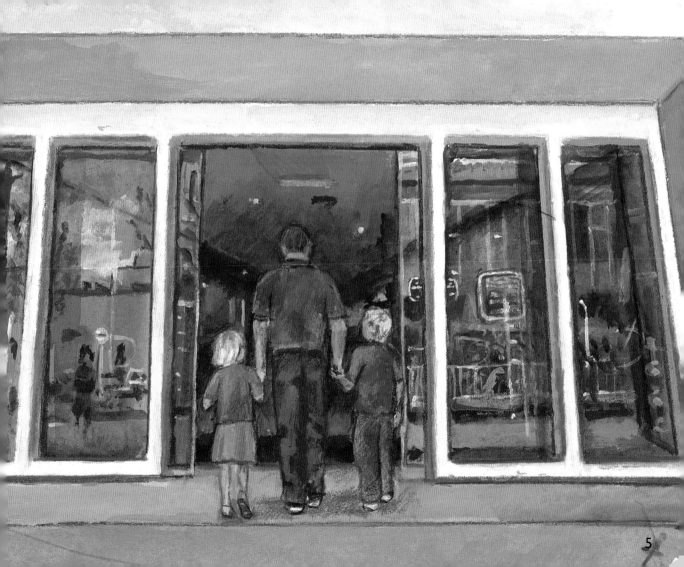

We went

in the helicopter.

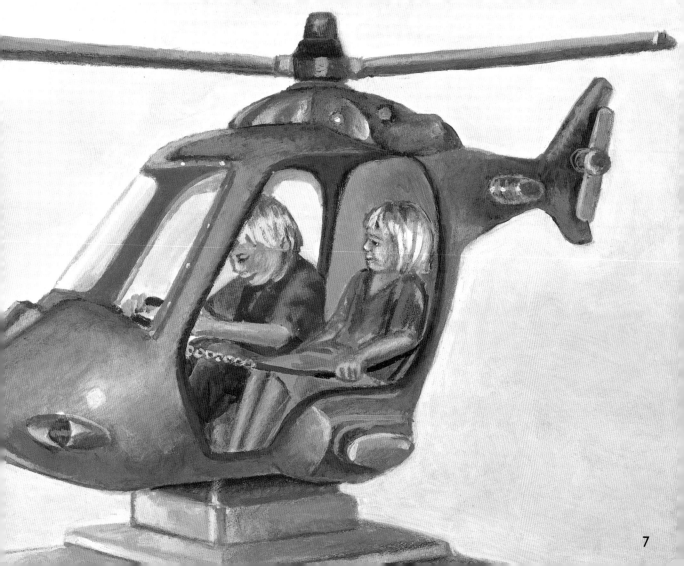

We went

to the book shop.

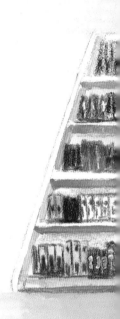

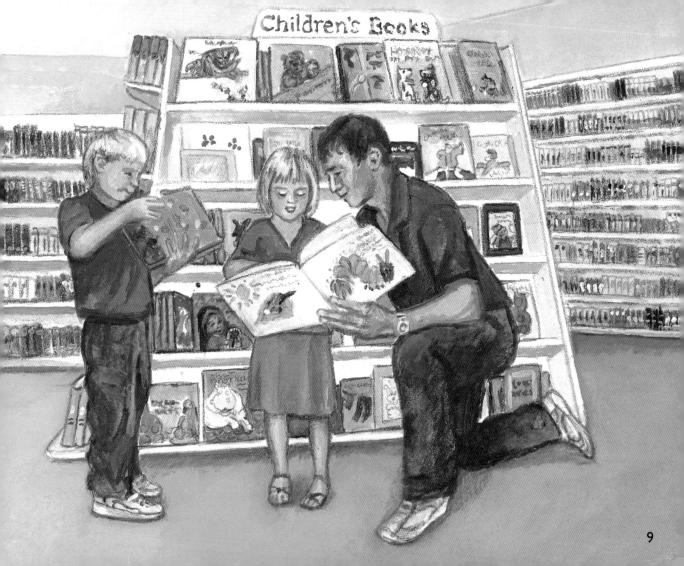

We went

to the shoe shop.

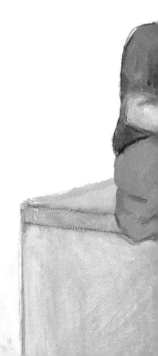

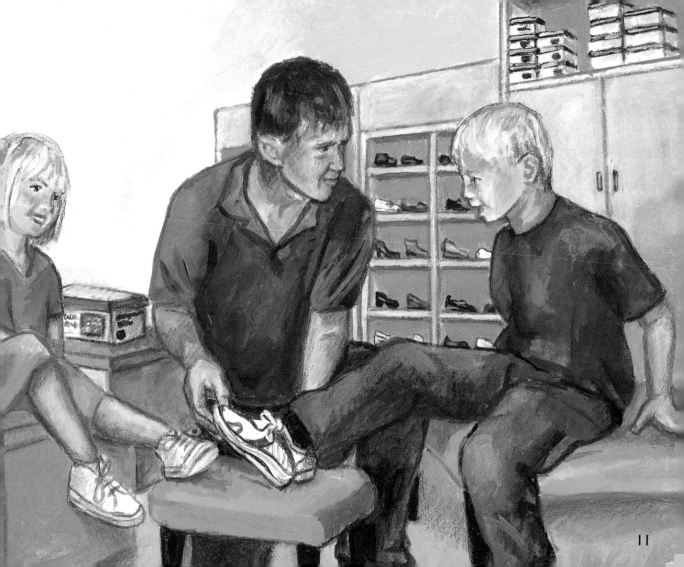

We went

to the toy shop.

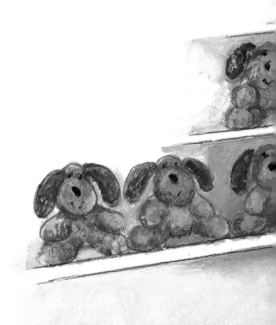

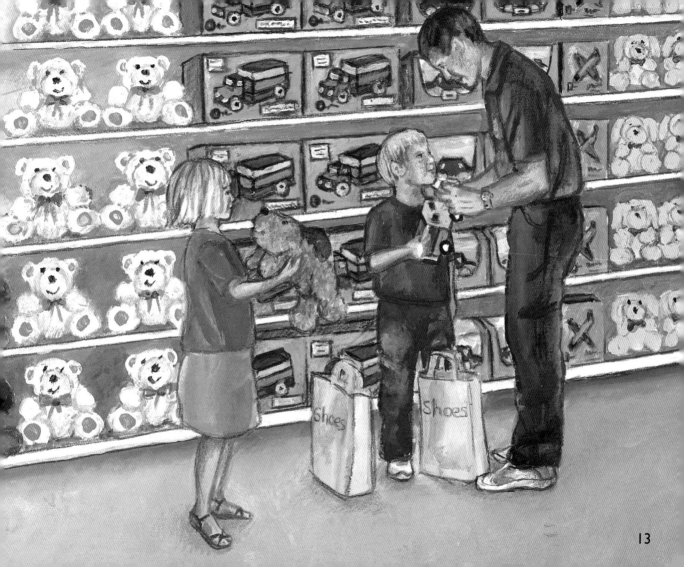

We went

to the ice-cream shop.

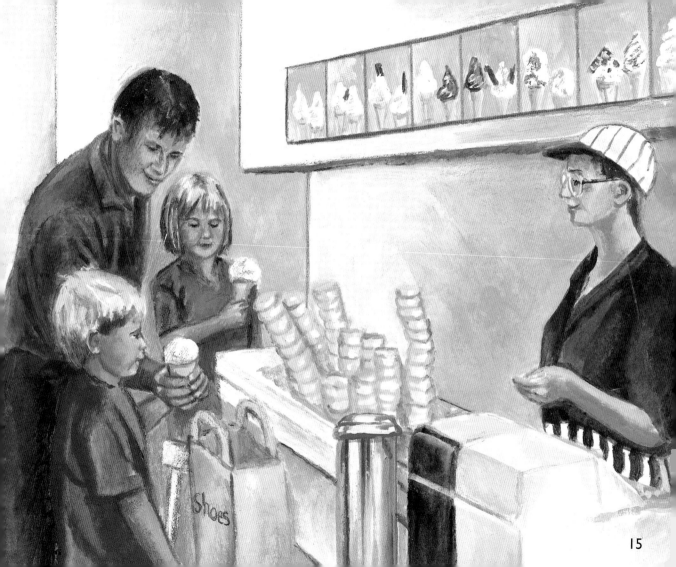

We went home.

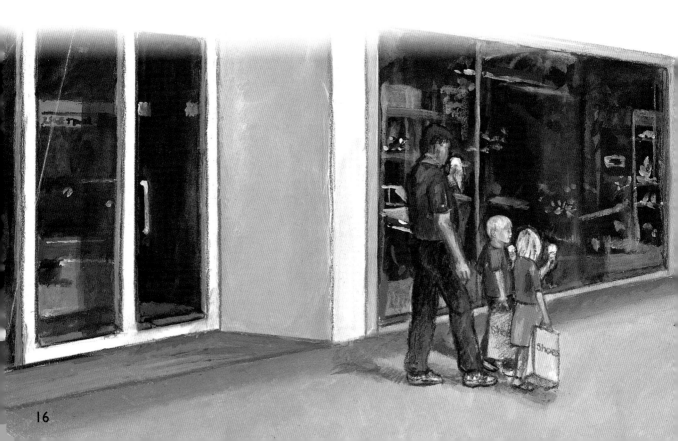